Hello Kitty's
Snowy Sports Spectacular

By Kris Hirschmann
Illustrated by Sachiho Hino

SCHOLASTIC INC.

New York   Toronto   London   Auckland   Sydney
Mexico City   New Delhi   Hong Kong   Buenos Aires

Decorate all of the
pictures in this book with
stickers. The page numbers
on the sticker page will
help you figure out which
stickers to use.

ISBN-13: 978-0-545-00347-6
ISBN-10: 0-545-00347-4

12 11 10 9 8 7 6 5 4 3 2 1   8 9 10 11 12/0

Designed by Angela Jun
Printed in the U.S.A.
First printing, February 2008

Contents

Chapter 1
Stuck Indoors

Friday afternoon had finally arrived. In Mr. Bearly's classroom, the students stared at the clock on the wall. *Tick . . . tick . . . tick . . . RRRRRING!* School was over for the week!

"Hooray!" cried the class. The students jumped up from their desks. They talked happily as they packed up their things. Everyone was excited about the weekend ahead.

Hello Kitty wasn't ready to leave. She walked over to the window and gazed outside. She saw snow and ice everywhere.

"Another boring weekend, stuck indoors," Hello Kitty sighed. "I'm so tired of winter!"

Kathy overheard what her friend said. She walked over to Hello Kitty and gave her a hug.

"Winter isn't boring, Hello Kitty," she said. "There are lots of things to do when it's snowy outside."

"Like what?" asked Hello Kitty.

"Like skiing," replied Kathy. "That's my favorite winter sport!"

"I don't know how to ski," Hello Kitty said.

"It's easy! I can teach you," said Kathy. "Why don't you come with me tomorrow? I have extra ski gear you can borrow. It'll be fun!"

Hello Kitty imagined herself on skis, whooshing

down a snowy hill. It *did* sound like fun. "Do you really think I could learn?" she said to her friend.

"Of course," Kathy replied. "You'll do great. In fact, I bet you'll be showing *me* some tricks by the end of the day. You're going to love winter sports. Just wait and see!"

Hello Kitty's
Winter Plans:

Stay indoors
Watch TV
Read books
Try to stay warm

Did You Know?

The Winter Olympics is a competition for the world's best winter athletes. It takes place once every four years. Many different countries have hosted this event.

Chapter 2
Downhill Slide

The next morning, Hello Kitty met Kathy at the skiing hill. Kathy showed her friend how to put on ski boots, skis, and ʃnoɯ goggles. She gave her two ski poles, one for each hand.

Finally Hello Kitty was ready.

"Just follow me. Do whatever I do," Kathy said. Then she started to ski slowly down the hill.

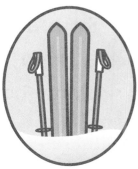

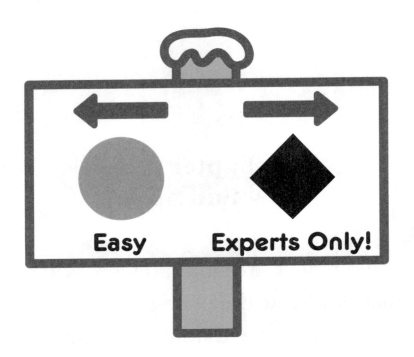

Easy   **Experts Only!**

Hello Kitty used her ski poles to push off. She was nervous at first.

But soon she started to feel more confident. She skied faster and faster. She even started to zigzag back and forth down the hill.

Soon Hello Kitty was zipping along behind Kathy. She laughed with delight. "This is fun!" she shouted.

But suddenly Hello Kitty started to pick up speed. She was going a little *too* fast. She tried to slow down—but she couldn't! Soon she was plummeting down the snowy slope.

"Help me!" she cried as she zoomed past Kathy. "I don't know how to stop!"

Kathy raced after her friend. Soon she had caught up with Hello Kitty. She threw her arms around Hello Kitty's waist and turned her skis sideways. Both friends slid to a halt right by their friend Thomas.

"That was fun!" said Kathy, giggling. "Let's do it again!"

Hello Kitty shook her head. "I don't think so," she said. "Skiing is too scary for me. I need a sport that doesn't go downhill."

" I can solve your problem," Thomas chimed in. "Come with me. I'll teach you the perfect winter sport!"

Hello Kitty's Notes to Self

Rule #1 in any fast sport:
Before you **go**,
learn how to **stop**!!

Did You Know?

Top skiers sometimes go faster than 60 miles
per hour (97 kph). That's as fast
as a car on a big highway!

Chapter 3
Fast Ice

Thomas led Hello Kitty to a large, icy pond. He handed her a pair of heavy black ice skates and a helmet.

"Put these on. We're going to play hockey," he said.

Soon Hello Kitty and Thomas were wearing their gear. They grabbed hockey sticks and a puck. Then they skated to the middle of the pond.

Thomas pointed at a net on one side of the ice. "That's the goal, Hello Kitty," he said. "Use your stick to hit the puck into that net."

Hello Kitty hit the puck hard. The black disk skidded across the pond and sailed into the net.

"Woo-hoo!" hooted Thomas. "You're a natural, Hello Kitty!"

Hello Kitty just smiled. She skated over to the goal. She put her stick into the goal and pulled out the puck. "Try to get it away from me," she said to Thomas.

In a flash, Thomas was by Hello Kitty's side. He reached for the puck with his stick. Hello Kitty turned, spun, and dodged. She kept the puck just out of Thomas's reach.

"You can't get it," she teased.

"Oh, yes I can!" Thomas said, laughing. He lifted his stick and lunged forward. **WHACK!** The stick smacked right into Hello Kitty's shin!

"**OUCH!!**" yelled Hello Kitty. She stopped skating. She reached down and rubbed her sore leg.

"I'm so sorry," cried Thomas. "I didn't mean to hit you."

"I know. It was an accident," said Hello Kitty. "I guess that's what happens when you play with sticks. Maybe hockey isn't the right sport for me, either."

Hockey Terms

Rink: The icy game surface

Puck: The black rubber disk

Stick: A curved wooden club used to hit the puck

Goal: The net into which players try to hit the puck

Shoot: To hit the puck toward the goal

Did You Know?

Hockey is the official national winter sport of Canada. It is the most-watched sport in Finland.

Chapter 4
In a Spin

Just then, Fifi skated over wearing a sparkly outfit with matching earmuffs. She wore dainty white skates on her feet.

"Oh! You look so pretty," said Hello Kitty.

"I have another outfit and more skates in my bag," Fifi said. "Would you like to figure skate with me?"

"I'd love to!" cried Hello Kitty.

Hello Kitty changed into Fifi's

extra outfit. Then she followed Fifi
to the edge of the pond. She slid her
feet into Fifi's skates, stood up, and
skated onto the icy pond.

"Whee! This is fun!" she said.
She glided gracefully across the
frozen surface.

"Watch this, Hello Kitty!" Fifi called across the pond. She stuck her arms out. Then she pulled them inward. As she did, she started to spin. Soon she was twirling so fast that her skirt stuck straight out from her body.

"Wow! I want to try that!" said Hello Kitty.

Hello Kitty stuck her arms out, just like Fifi. She pulled them inward. Then she started to spin.

"Good job, Hello Kitty!" yelled Fifi.

But Hello Kitty was already slowing down. "Ohhhh, my head," she moaned as she spun to a stop.

She sat right down on the ice and closed her eyes.

Fifi skated over as fast as she could. "Are you okay?" she asked.

"I'm just dizzy," Hello Kitty replied. "And maybe a little bit discouraged, too. Figure skating isn't for me. I'm afraid I'll never find a winter sport I really like!"

Hello Kitty's Notes to Self

Ice-skating is harder than
it looks. I'll spin more
slowly next time!

Did You Know?

Figure skating jumps have some interesting
names. Flips, lutzes, loops, salchows,
and axels are a few of the jumps
used in competitions.

Chapter 5
Walking on Snow

Fifi helped Hello Kitty to stand up. She led her to the edge of the pond, where they found Jody waiting for them. He wore something funny on each foot. They looked like saucers. In his hands, he held another pair of saucers.

"What are those?" asked Hello Kitty.

"They're snowshoes," Jody replied. "We can use them to walk on soft snow. Do you want to try it?"

"Hmmm . . . walking is slow, no sticks are involved, and you don't need to spin. That sounds perfect," said Hello Kitty. "Count me in!"

Hello Kitty bent down and strapped the snowshoes to her feet. She took a few careful steps onto a fluffy snow pile. She thought the pile might break under her weight . . . but it didn't!

"Neat!" she said with a grin.

"Follow me, Hello Kitty," said Jody. "Let's go for a walk!"

The friends tramped away from the pond. The snow under their feet got deeper and deeper. It bent

and squeaked with every step. But it didn't break.

Soon Hello Kitty and Jody reached a forest. "Snowshoeing is wonderful! And this forest is beautiful," Hello Kitty said to herself. She tilted her head back so she could look at the treetops.

Hello Kitty didn't see the tree root sticking out of the snow. Her snowshoe slid under the root. **WHOOPS!** Hello Kitty tripped and fell . . . right into a deep snowbank!

Hello Kitty tried to jump up, but she couldn't. The snow hole was too deep. She wiggled her arms and legs around, trying to escape. But

the more Hello Kitty wiggled, the deeper she sank.

"Help! I'm stuck!" she cried.

Ingredients for Cocoa:

Chocolate
Cinnamon
Nutmeg
Brown sugar

Did You Know?

Rabbits called snowshoe hares have built-in
"snowshoes." Their big back feet keep
them from sinking into the snow.

Chapter 6
Snow Angels

Jody heard Hello Kitty's cry for help. So did Kathy, Thomas, and Fifi, who were ʃnowshoeing nearby. Everyone rushed to the edge of the hole.

"We'll save you, Hello Kitty!" they said.

The friends found a big stick lying in the ʃnow. They held on to one end of the stick and poked the other end into the hole. Hello Kitty grabbed the stick and held on tight.

"One . . . two . . . three . . . PULL!"
said the friends. They yanked on
the stick. Out popped a very cold
and Snowy Hello Kitty.

"Are you OK?" asked Jody.

"I guess so. I'm not hurt," said
Hello Kitty. "But I'm fed up with

winter sports! I'm not good at anything."

"That's not true, Hello Kitty. You're *really* good at one thing," said Kathy. "Look!"

Kathy pointed at the place where Hello Kitty had fallen. There in the snow was the best snow angel anyone had ever seen.

"Oooooh!" cried the friends. "Let's make more!"

The friends took turns falling into the deep snow. They wiggled their arms and legs. When they were done, the other friends used the stick to pull them out. Soon four more snow angels had appeared.

Thomas looked at the angel-shaped holes. "These *snow* angels are great, Hello Kitty," he said. "Thanks for showing us how to make them!"

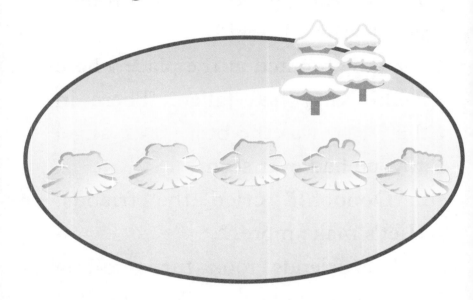

Hello Kitty blushed and smiled. She felt warm and happy inside. Her friends had taught her so many fun things. It felt good to show *them*

something for a change.

"I think I've finally found the perfect winter sport," she said with a shy grin.

Chapter 7
Snowy Souvenirs

Suddenly Hello Kitty realized that she was shivering. She looked at her friends. They were shivering, too.

"We need to warm up," she said. "Let's go back to my house. We'll have some hot cocoa . . . and I'll teach you something fun while we drink it."

"Hooray! Let's go!" cheered the friends.

Everyone trooped back to Hello

Kitty's house. Mama poured them steaming mugs of cocoa. Then they went into Hello Kitty's playroom.

Hello Kitty went to her craft table. She got out paper plates, scissors, tape, and markers. She carefully cut a paper plate. Then she bent it around and taped it. The plate looked just like an angel.

"Oh! How cute!" said the friends.

Hello Kitty made four more angels. She used a gold marker to color the angels' wings and halos. Next she drew faces and hair on all five angels. Then she drew skis on the first angel, hockey skates on the second angel, figure skates on the third angel, and snowshoes on the fourth. She handed the angels to Kathy, Thomas, Fifi, and Jody. She kept the last angel for herself.

"These *snow* angels will remind us of our *snowy sports* day," she said.

"Thank you, Hello Kitty!" said everyone.

"No, thank *you*," replied Hello Kitty. "I learned something important today. Everyone is great at *something*— even me! Besides, I don't have to be a *sports* expert to have fun with my friends. I just need to take things a little slower. And . . . I need lots of practice! Can we try again?"

"Of course!" said her friends.

"I knew you would love winter sports," Kathy added.

Hello Kitty smiled at her friend. "You were right," she said. "I *do* love winter sports. I think I could even get pretty good at them. But no matter what happens, I know one thing for sure. Snowy days aren't boring at all. They're the perfect time for fun and friendship!"

Hello Kitty's Snow Angels

You can make snow angels, just like the ones Hello Kitty made!

You need:
- A paper plate
- Scissors
- Tape
- Markers or crayons

What you do:

1. Cut the paper plate along the dotted lines as shown in the picture. You don't need the shaded parts of the plate. You can throw them away.

2. Draw a face on the angel. Color the angel's wings and halo.

3. Decorate the angel's robe any way you like.

4. Bend the paper plate backward so edge A overlaps edge B. Use tape to stick the edges together.

5. Set the angel on a flat surface. Bend the head and wings so they stand straight up. Your snow angel is done!

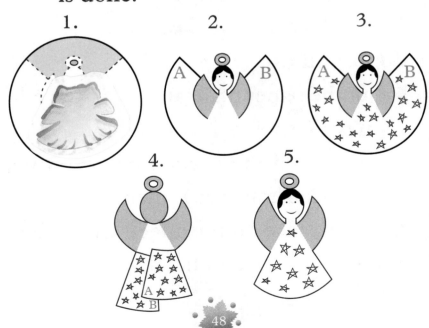

1.

2.

3.

4.

5.

Chapter 1 — page 4

Chapter 2 — page 10

Chapter 3 — page 16

Chapter 4 — page 22

© 1976, 2008 Sanrio CO, LTD. Used under license
ISBN: S-T15-00347-4